Note to Librarians, Teachers, and Parents:

Blastoff! Readers are carefully developed by literacy experts and combine standards-based content with developmentally appropriate text.

Level 1 provides the most support through repetition of high-frequency words, light text, predictable sentence patterns, and strong visual support.

Level 2 offers early readers a bit more challenge through varied simple sentences, increased text load, and less repetition of high-frequency words.

Level 3 advances early-fluent readers toward fluency through increased text and concept load, less reliance on visuals, longer sentences, and more literary language.

Level 4 builds reading stamina by providing more text per page, increased use of punctuation, greater variation in sentence patterns, and increasingly challenging vocabulary.

Level 5 encourages children to move from "learning to read" to "reading to learn" by providing even more text, varied writing styles, and less familiar topics.

Whichever book is right for your reader, Blastoff! Readers are the perfect books to build confidence and encourage a love of reading that will last a lifetime!

This edition first published in 2020 by Bellwether Media, Inc.

No part of this publication may be reproduced in whole or in part without written permission of the publisher. For information regarding permission, write to Bellwether Media, Inc., Attention: Permissions Department, 6012 Blue Circle Drive, Minnetonka, MN 55343.

Library of Congress Cataloging-in-Publication Data

Names: Shaffer, Lindsay, author.
Title: Snow Leopards / by Lindsay Shaffer.
Description: Minneapolis, MN : Bellwether Media, Inc., [2020] |
  Series: Blastoff! Readers: Animals of the Mountains | Includes bibliographical references and index. |
  Audience: Age 5-8. | Audience: K to Grade 3.
Identifiers: LCCN 2018060791 (print) | LCCN 2019001619 (ebook) | ISBN 9781618915580 (ebook) |
  ISBN 9781644870174 (hardcover : alk. paper)
Subjects: LCSH: Snow leopard--Juvenile literature.
Classification: LCC QL737.C23 (ebook) | LCC QL737.C23 S5118 2020 (print) | DDC 599.75/55--dc23
LC record available at https://lccn.loc.gov/2018060791

Text copyright © 2020 by Bellwether Media, Inc. BLASTOFF! READERS and associated logos are trademarks and/or registered trademarks of Bellwether Media, Inc. SCHOLASTIC, CHILDREN'S PRESS, and associated logos are trademarks and/or registered trademarks of Scholastic Inc., 557 Broadway, New York, NY 10012.

Editor: Kate Moening   Designer: Jeffrey Kollock

Printed in the United States of America, North Mankato, MN

Table of Contents

Life in the Mountains	4
Leaving Signs	12
Leaping Leopards	16
Glossary	22
To Learn More	23
Index	24

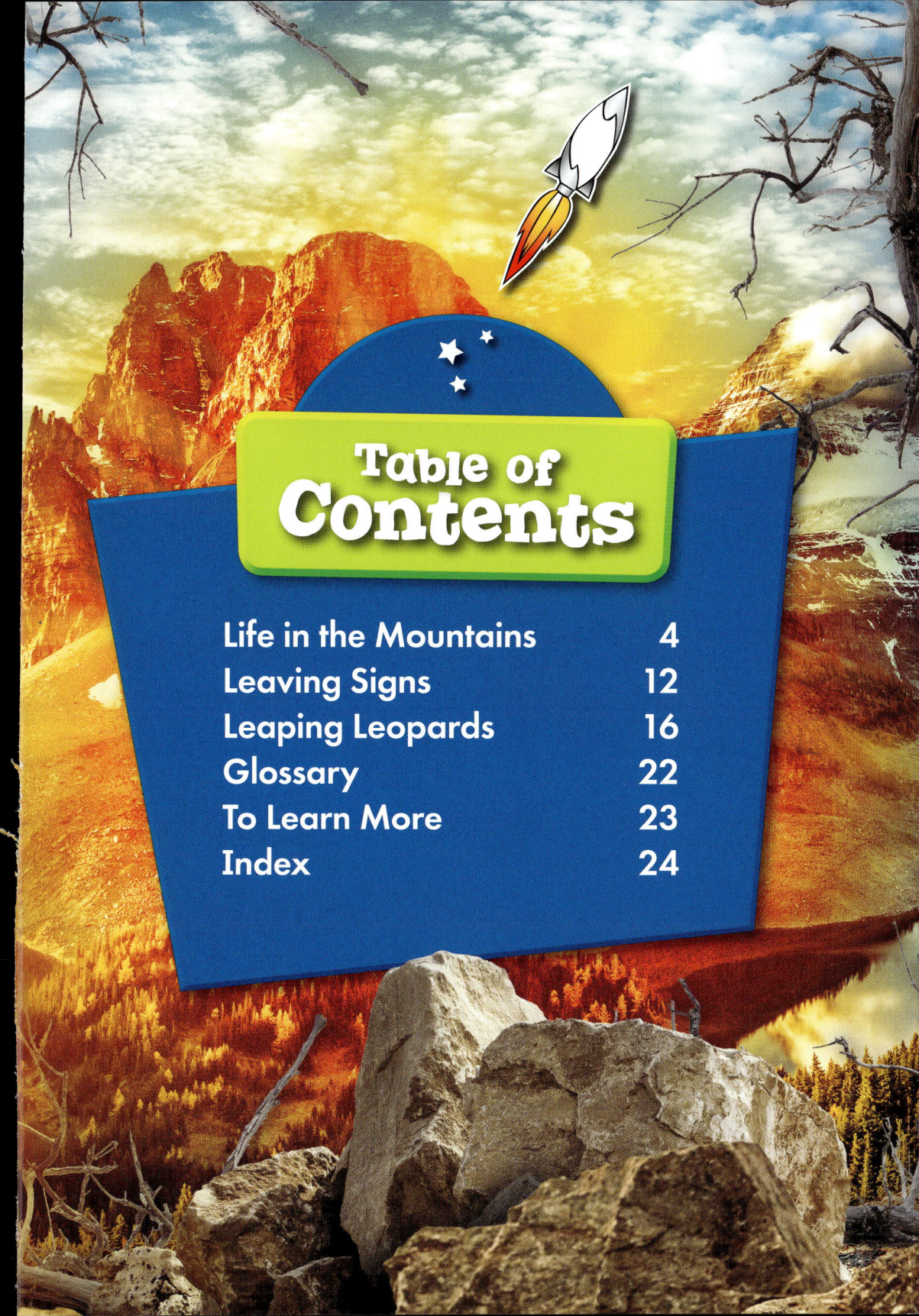

Life in the Mountains

Snow leopards live high in the mountains of central Asia.

Special **adaptations** help them survive in this chilly **biome**.

Snow Leopard Range

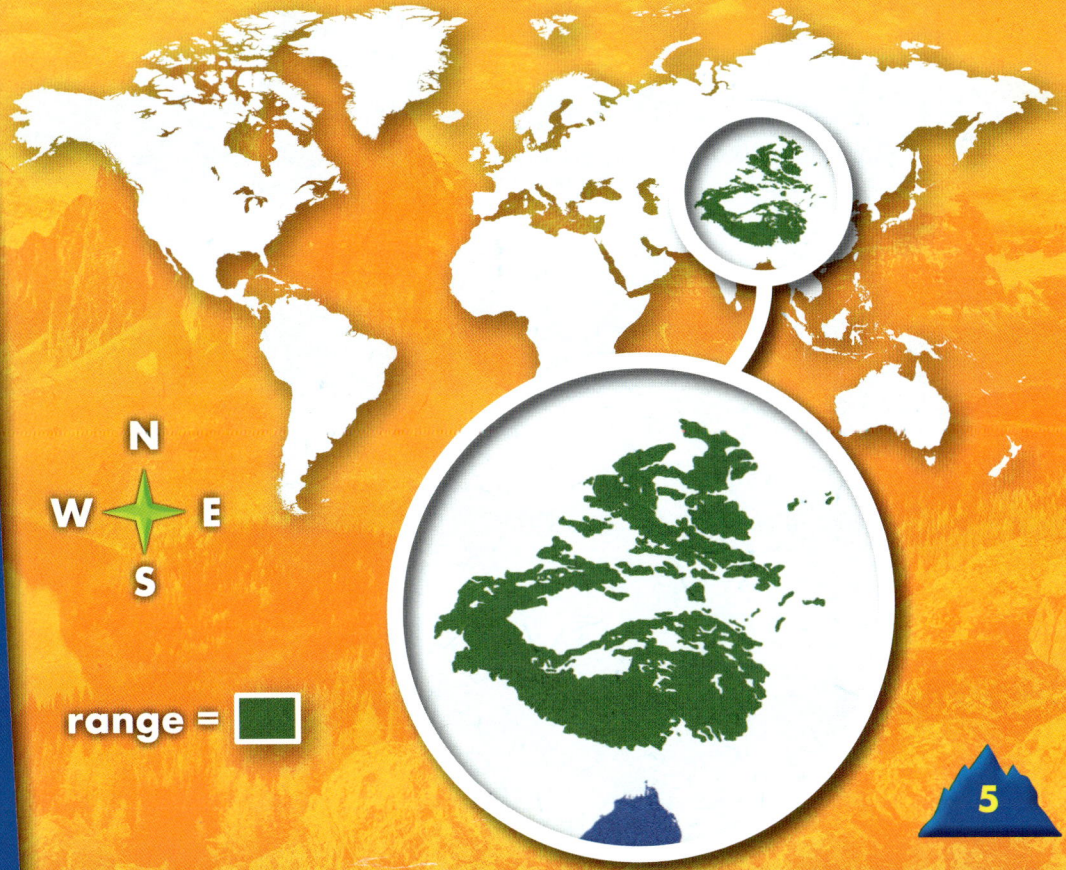

range = ▢

Snow leopards have thick **coats**. Their belly fur grows extra long to keep them warm!

These coats also change with the seasons. They grow thicker and lighter-colored in winter.

Snow Leopard Stats

| Least Concern | Near Threatened | Vulnerable | Endangered | Critically Endangered | Extinct in the Wild | Extinct |

conservation status: vulnerable

life span: about 12 years

Large paws help snow leopards walk easily over snow.

Long tails help the leopards **balance** on rocks. These **mammals** use their fluffy tails as blankets, too!

Mountain air is thin and cold. Strong lungs help snow leopards take big breaths.

Special Adaptations

long, fluffy tail

wide nose

large, furry paws

Wide noses warm the air before it gets to their lungs.

Leaving Signs

It is hard to find enough food in the mountains. Snow leopards are **solitary** to make it easier.

Their **territories** cover around 80 square miles (207 square kilometers)!

Snow leopards mark their territories by leaving signs.

marking territory

They rub their cheeks on rocks.
They scratch the ground.
They spray pee, too!

Leaping Leopards

Snow leopards are powerful **predators**.

They hunt **prey** up to three times their own weight!

Snow Leopard Diet

ibex

woolly hares

blue sheep

Snow leopards sneak up on prey. **Rosettes** help them blend in with rocks.

When they get close, they **pounce**! These big cats can leap up to 50 feet (15 meters).

rosettes

Snow leopards hunt in early morning and evening. The dim light helps hide them from prey.

These cats are top predators in their mountain biome!

Glossary

adaptations—changes an animal undergoes over a long period of time to fit where it lives

balance—moving or staying in the same place without losing control or falling

biome—a large area with certain plants, animals, and weather

coats—the hair or fur covering some animals

mammals—warm-blooded animals that have backbones and feed their young milk

pounce—to suddenly jump on something to catch it

predators—animals that hunt other animals for food

prey—animals that are hunted by other animals for food

rosettes—dark spots on a snow leopard's coat

solitary—living alone

territories—land areas where animals live

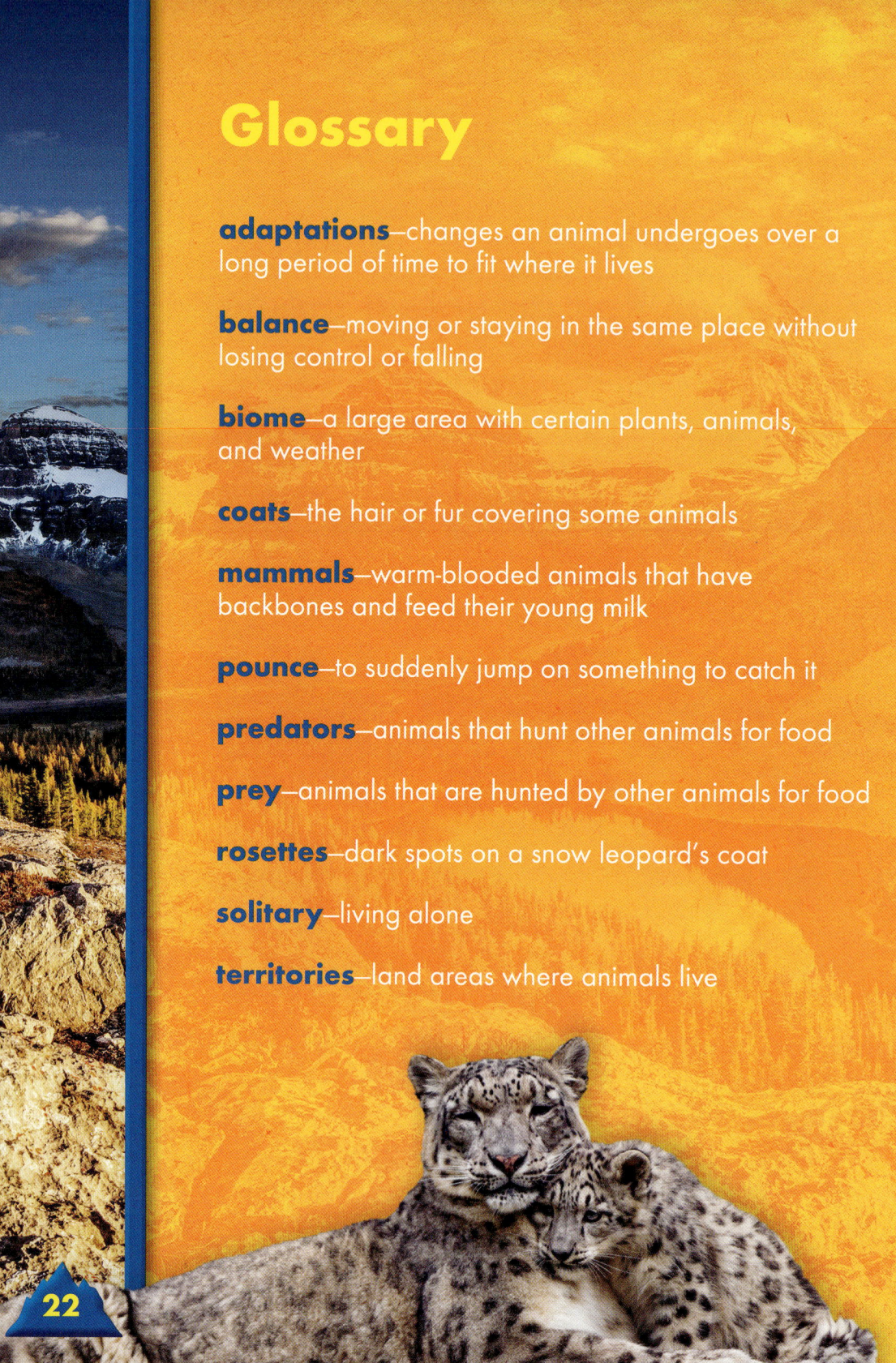

To Learn More

AT THE LIBRARY
Bodden, Valerie. *Snow Leopards*. Mankato, Minn.: Creative Education and Creative Paperbacks, 2018.

Carr, Aaron. *Snow Leopard*. New York, N.Y.: AV2 by Weigl, 2017.

Rissman, Rebecca. *Kings of the Mountains*. North Mankato, Minn.: Capstone Press, 2018.

ON THE WEB

FACTSURFER

Factsurfer.com gives you a safe, fun way to find more information.

1. Go to www.factsurfer.com.

2. Enter "snow leopards" into the search box and click 🔍.

3. Select your book cover to see a list of related web sites.

Index

adaptations, 5, 11
Asia, 4
balance, 9
biome, 5, 21
cheeks, 15
coats, 6
food, 12, 17
fur, 6, 11
hunt, 17, 20
leap, 18
lungs, 10, 11
mammals, 9
noses, 11
paws, 8, 11
pee, 15
pounce, 18
predators, 16, 21
prey, 17, 18, 20
range, 4, 5
rosettes, 18

seasons, 6
snow, 8
solitary, 12
status, 7
tails, 9, 11
territories, 13, 14, 15

The images in this book are reproduced through the courtesy of: Z Kerth, front cover; Dennis W Donohue, pp. 4-5; imageBROKER/ Alamy, p. 6; Ondrej Chvatal, pp. 6-7; Warren Metcalf, pp. 8-9, 11 (leopard); Andy Rouse/ Nature Picture Library, p. 9; Don Johnston_MA/ Alamy, pp. 10-11; chbaum, p. 11 (paw); Pantheon, pp. 12-13; Evelyn D. Harrison, p. 14; Steve Winter/ National Geographic Image Collection, pp. 14-15; Andy Poole, pp. 16-17; Yuriy Bartenev, p. 17 (ibex); Ovchinnikova Irina, p. 17 (hare); Yongyut Kumsri, p. 17 (sheep); Vladimir Sazonov, p. 18; Abeselom Zerit, pp. 18-19; Benjamin B, p. 19; Tambako the Jaguar, pp. 20, 22